EYEWITNESS CLASSICS

20,000 LEAGUES UNDER THE SEA

A DORLING KINDERSLEY BOOK

A RETELLING OF JULES VERNE'S
20,000 Leagues Under the Sea FOR YOUNG READERS

Project Editor Natascha Biebow
Project Art Editor Mark Regardsoe
Designer Tanya Tween
Senior Editors Alastair Dougall and Marie Greenwood
Managing Art Editor Jacquie Gulliver
Research Fergus Day
Picture Research Catherine Costelloe
Production Steve Lang and Katy Holmes
DTP Designers Kim Browne and Sarah Williams

First Published in Great Britain in 1998 by
Dorling Kindersley Limited, 9 Henrietta Street, London WC2E 8PS

Visit us on the World Wide Web at http://www.dk.com

A CIP catalogue record for this book is available from the British Library.

ISBN 0-7513-7073-8

Colour reproduction by Bright Arts in Hong Kong
Printed by Graphicom in Italy

EYEWITNESS ◉ CLASSICS

20,000 LEAGUES UNDER THE SEA

JULES VERNE
Retold by RON MILLER

Illustrated by
PAUL WRIGHT

DK

DORLING KINDERSLEY
LONDON • NEW YORK • STUTTGART • MOSCOW

Contents

The *Nautilus*

Captain Nemo

Ned Land

Conseil

Professor Aronnax

INTRODUCTION

J ULES VERNE WAS A PIONEER of science fiction, a visionary whose ideas have enthralled generations. His extraordinary adventure stories have transported readers to every corner of the world, from the depths of the oceans to the centre of the Earth, and even into outer space. Perhaps the greatest and best-known of these is *20,000 Leagues Under the Sea*. From its publication in 1870, the fantastic submarine *Nautilus*, the enigmatic Captain Nemo, and the amazing undersea world of the novel have thrilled audiences the world over.

Verne was fascinated by science and technology, and one of the key strengths of his stories is their solid factual basis. Inspired by 19th-century submarine inventions, the *Nautilus* is uncannily prophetic of modern technological developments, such as the nuclear submarine. Indeed, many of Verne's fantastical machines were based on such sound ideas that they inspired inventors to try and duplicate them.

This Eyewitness Classic edition has been edited and revised for younger readers, while retaining all the excitement of the original novel. A unique cross-section of the *Nautilus* and a map of the characters' journey, together with diagrams, engravings, and colour photographs introduce the reader to the rich underwater world of the *Nautilus* and provide additional information about submarines, diving, and oceanography. So welcome aboard the *Nautilus*, and be prepared for the journey of a lifetime, 20,000 leagues around the world!

Mapping the characters' journey

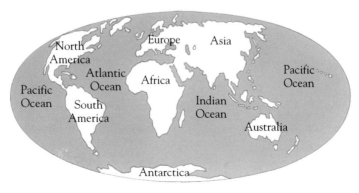

Look out for this map as the story unfolds. It shows the route of the characters' journey, and how far they have travelled.
1 league = 3 nautical miles = 5.6 km (18,400 ft)

The Scotia
Before planes, passenger ships were the only transport across the Atlantic. In 1866, the Scotia was the fastest. If it had been damaged, as in Verne's story, there would have been a huge uproar.

Chapter One

HUNT FOR THE MONSTER

THE YEAR 1866 was a memorable one. Ships at sea had been sighting a mysterious "thing", a long, pointed, glowing object that travelled at impossible speeds. Everyone talked about it, every newspaper wrote about it, and scientists argued over what the "sea monster" might be. Most of them agreed that it must be some unknown type of animal, perhaps a kind of whale. The suggestion that it might be a submarine boat was laughed at. Who could possibly have built such a thing? It would be beyond the resources of even the richest nation, even if it could be kept a secret.

People stopped laughing and took the matter more seriously when a passenger ship belonging to the famed Cunard line, the *Scotia*, was rammed by the monster. A huge hole was torn in the side of the ship and it was barely able to limp back to port without sinking. When the *Scotia* was raised out of the water for repairs, the mystery deepened.

The hole was a perfect triangle, as though it had been punched by a machine! What kind of animal could do such a thing? Whatever it was, it was now known to be dangerous. There was a great hue and cry among the public, ship owners, and insurance companies for the American government to do something about this menace.

This was the state of affairs when I arrived in New York City. My name is Pierre Aronnax and I am a professor at the Museum of Natural History in Paris. Since I had just written a book about the sea, the newspapers wanted to know my opinion of the "sea monster". I told them that I thought that a giant narwhal had accidentally rammed the *Scotia* with its huge tusk. This interview helped convince the government of the reality of the creature and plans were made to send the frigate *Abraham Lincoln* – under the

Every newspaper was filled with news about the mysterious glowing object sighted at sea.

In my hotel room, Conseil and I read the shocking news about the ramming of the Scotia.

command of the famous Captain Farragut – in search of the sea monster.

I thought no more of the matter and my assistant Conseil and I were in our hotel room packing for our return to Paris when I received this surprising letter:

TO MR ARONNAX, PROFESSOR AT THE
PARIS MUSEUM OF NATURAL HISTORY,
FIFTH AVENUE HOTEL, NEW YORK

SIR - I HOPE YOU WILL CONSENT
TO JOIN THE ABRAHAM LINCOLN'S EXPEDITION.
COMMANDER FARRAGUT HAS A CABIN AT YOUR DISPOSAL.
VERY CORDIALLY YOURS,

J. B. HOBSON, SECRETARY OF THE NAVY

Narwhal
Aronnax speculates that the hole in the Scotia was bored by the tusk of a giant narwhal. Related to the beluga whale, narwhals live in icy Arctic waters. Males have tusks as long as 3 m (10 ft).

Crow's nest

Bowsprit

Cannon

US naval frigate
Verne imagines that the "monster" becomes a threat to national security, so the American government sends a well-armed warship, called a frigate, to destroy it. Its captain, Commander Farragut, was a real hero in the American Civil War (1861-65).

New York Harbour ca. 1875

New York Harbour
New York Harbour is an important American port.

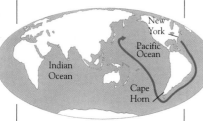

The *Abraham Lincoln*'s route

Conseil and I, along with a famous Canadian harpooner named Ned Land, soon found ourselves steaming out of New York Harbour on board the US naval frigate, the *Abraham Lincoln*. If anyone could find the monster, I was sure that Commander Farragut could. Either he would kill the narwhal or it would kill him. There was no third choice.

Just before we had sailed from New York, the monster had struck again in the Pacific Ocean. So this is where we headed. First, we had to make the long journey down the east coast of South America and through the treacherous waters of Cape Horn. Once the *Abraham Lincoln* reached the peaceful waters of the Pacific, we cruised for months without catching so much as a glimpse of the monster. Where was it?

After three months, the crew grew very impatient and there was a great deal of grumbling. The captain posted a $2,000 reward for the first person to see the monster, but even this didn't help the eyes or the mood of the crew.

I became good friends with Ned, whom I found to be a bold, passionate man. Conseil and I passed the days arguing with him about what kind of creature the monster might be. Ned, an experienced whaler, flatly refused to accept my theory that it was a giant narwhal. I tried to prove to him that something like that was possible, but all he would say was, "Pooh! You'll never convince me that a narwhal could punch a hole in an iron ship!"

Finally, the captain said that if the monster wasn't sighted within three days, he'd turn the ship back to New York.

Two days passed and still we saw nothing but empty ocean. But on the evening of the third day, Conseil and I were leaning

on the starboard railing, when we heard
Ned shout from the crow's nest: "Ahoy! It's the thing itself!"

Not far from the ship, we made out a strange glow in the water.
Suddenly, two jets of spray shot into the air and I was sure that my
theory was right: the monster was spouting like some kind of whale.

While Ned climbed onto the bowsprit with his harpoon to get a
clear throw, the captain gave an order and a cannon was fired. I saw
the shell ricochet from the monster's glistening black back. Then,
all of a sudden, the creature turned and rushed towards us! I saw Ned
throw his harpoon. There was a tremendous *crash!*
and I was thrown overboard. The last thing I
remember is the water closing over my head.

Harpoon

*At the time of this story,
whaling was an important
industry. Whales were hunted
for their oil and bone by
harpooners like Ned. His skill
with a harpoon makes him a
key member of the team sent
to kill the sea monster.*

*Ned braced himself
on the bowsprit and
aimed his harpoon
at the monster.*

I would have drowned if Conseil had not jumped in after me and pulled me to the surface. I looked around for the *Abraham Lincoln*. To my horror, it was moving slowly away.

"Why aren't they trying to save us?" I cried.

"The rudder and propeller are broken," Conseil replied. "They're helpless."

"Then we're lost!"

We drifted for hours in the dark, taking turns keeping each other afloat. Near one o'clock in the morning, I was seized by a dreadful fatigue. I begged Conseil to leave me, but he refused to abandon his master. Still, I knew he could not hold me up for much longer. I had almost given up hope for both of us when I thought I heard a voice.

"Did you hear that, Conseil?"

"Yes! It's someone calling!"

Conseil towed me towards the voice. My hands struck something hard. I looked up and saw a familiar face. It was Ned! A few moments later he was hauling us out of the water.

A hatch suddenly opened and several masked men appeared.

"What are we standing on?" I asked.

"Your narwhal," Ned replied, "a narwhal made of sheet iron!"

I looked down. The black surface we stood on was made of smooth, polished, riveted iron plates. The monster was some kind of machine!

"If this is a submarine," I said, "then there must be a crew."

"We're saved!" said Conseil.

"I wouldn't be so sure of that," replied Ned, looking towards a hatch that had suddenly opened. Several masked men appeared, and forced us down into their mysterious vessel.

We were taken to a cell and locked inside. The only light came from a brightly glowing half-globe on the ceiling.

"At least we can see," said Ned.

"But we're still in the dark about ourselves," I replied.

"Well, I have my bowie knife and can see well enough to use it!" said Ned.

I heard someone unlocking our prison door. "Don't do anything hasty, Ned!" I warned.

A steward entered our cell carrying a tray of dishes. I spoke to him in French, but he didn't reply. Ned tried English and Conseil German, but still the man did not respond. Another man brought in fresh clothes, while the steward silently laid out our table.

"What do you suppose it is?" I wondered, looking at the steaming dishes.

"Fillet of shark, I would imagine," replied Ned.

Whatever it was, the food looked delicious and we ate like starving men. I noticed that all the silver knives and forks bore a strange crest: an "N" with a Latin saying, "*Mobilis in Mobile*". It must be the submarine captain's motto.

Our appetites satisfied, we were all overcome by a strange drowsiness. As I wondered whether our food had been drugged, I fell into a deep, dreamless sleep.

We were all frozen by the sound of a powerful voice.

When I awoke, a draught of fresh sea air was coming through a vent above the door. I breathed deeply, and looked around our iron-walled cell. There didn't seem to be much else to do but discuss our predicament. Hot-headed Ned complained bitterly – he even complained that Conseil wasn't complaining!

"What's the use of complaining?" replied Conseil, as calm as ever.

"It does you good to complain! At least you're doing something! If these pirates think they can keep me locked up in this iron box for long, they've another thing coming! How about you, Professor?"

"I think we've stumbled onto a secret we weren't

meant to discover. Someone may consider that our lives are less important than keeping this secret."

"Unless whoever it is enlists us in his crew," offered Conseil.

"Or unless some other warship is more successful than the *Abraham Lincoln* in sinking this nest of pirates," added Ned. "There's only one thing we can do."

"What?" I asked.

"Escape!"

"Escaping from a prison would be difficult enough – but escaping from an underwater prison?"

"Well," Ned replied, "we'll just have to take over the ship!"

"Impossible!" I cried.

"We'll see about that!"

"I know your temper, Ned. Promise not to do anything unless the time is right, or you'll just make things even worse for us."

"I promise," Ned said, but I didn't feel very reassured.

Hours passed and we were getting hungrier and hungrier, for there had been no food since the meal of the day before. Despite his promise, Ned was becoming angrier and angrier, and I feared an explosion the next time he encountered a member of the crew.

Just then we heard steps on the metal floor outside. The lock turned and the door opened. The steward once more stepped into our cell.

Before I could stop him, Ned threw the man to the floor and seized him by the throat. Conseil tried to pull the harpooner away, and I was just coming to the steward's rescue, when we were all frozen by a powerful voice:

"Be quiet, Master Land! And you, Professor Aronnax, will you be so good as to listen to me?"

It was the commander of the submarine who had just spoken.

The submarine's motto
The Latin motto is the first clue about the friends' mysterious captors. The first word, "mobilis", refers to something mobile – the submarine. "In mobile" means in a constantly changing element – the sea. Aronnax wonders what the "N" in the crest stands for.

Treasures of art
*Nemo's salon, which may
have looked like this 19th-
century one, housed a
collection of valuable paintings
and rare books. Nemo shares
Verne's interest in science,
music, and natural history.*

Crab   Starfish

Coral   Shell

Treasures of nature
*Displayed in elegant glass
cases around the salon,
Nemo has collected marine
plants, animals, and shells.
Aronnax admires these
specimens, which were rare
and valuable in Europe at
the time.*

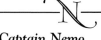

Captain Nemo
*The captain of the Nautilus
gives his name as "Nemo",
which means "no one".
He clearly wishes to keep
his identity a secret.*

Chapter two

THE NAUTILUS

THE COMMANDER OF THE *NAUTILUS* was a tall man with a broad forehead and widely spaced black eyes. Arms folded, he looked at us calmly. "An annoying circumstance," he said, "has brought you to trouble the existence of a man who has broken all ties with humanity."

"Accidentally!" I said.

"Was it an accident that the *Abraham Lincoln* fired at me?"

"We thought you were a sea monster."

"Wouldn't you also have shot at a submarine?"

I had no answer for that.

"You understand, then," he continued, "that I have the right to treat you as enemies?"

"But you are a civilized man, sir!"

"Professor," the captain replied with some anger, "I am not what you call a civilized man! I have done with society and its laws! Still, you are free to enjoy the liberty of the *Nautilus*."

"That's no more liberty than a prisoner has!" cried Ned.

"It will have to do, Master Land. Professor," the captain said, turning to me, "I know your work well and respect it, but you don't know everything. I promise that you won't regret your stay on the *Nautilus*. You will visit the land of marvels!"

"You know our names, sir," I said. "What are we to call you?"

"You may call me Captain Nemo."

The captain invited me to join him for breakfast in his quarters. Leaving my companions to enjoy their meal, I followed my host down a corridor and into a beautiful dining room. All the food on the table had come from the sea. We ate, then the captain told me something about his life and his marvellous ship.

"The sea supplies everything I need," he told me. "I love the sea! The sea is everything. Only here is independence. Here I recognize no masters. On the surface, men rule unjustly, but far below the waves, their power disappears. Here I am free!"

Nemo paused, and
motioned for me to follow him. "The parts of the *Nautilus* were
manufactured all over the world, then shipped to an island and
secretly assembled," he explained. "Through here is the grand

"I love the sea! Only here am I free," Nemo told me.

salon – a museum for which I have gathered treasures of art and nature. I also have a library
of twelve thousand books. These are the last souvenirs of a world that is dead to me."

Nemo offered me a seat and showed me a plan of the *Nautilus*. His cabin was in the bow; then
came the salon, library, and dining room, the cell in which Ned, Conseil, and I were held, the
galley, and the crew's quarters. The engine room was in the stern. The *Nautilus* was powered by
electricity and controlled by instruments in Nemo's cabin and in the pilot house.

THE NAUTILUS

In 1870, when Verne published *20,000 Leagues Under the Sea*, the *Nautilus* would have been considered an impossible dream. At the time, submarine inventors were trying out different ways of powering their craft and keeping them underwater for long periods of time. Using the latest scientific breakthroughs as a springboard, Verne created the ultimate submarine. The *Nautilus* could withstand incredible water pressure, stay underwater for as long as two days, and was completely powered by electricity, something unheard of in Verne's time.

NAUTILUS FACTS

- The *Nautilus* measures 70 m (230 ft) from bow to stern; it is 8 m- (26 ft-) wide.
- The *Nautilus* weighs 1,500 tons.
- When the *Nautilus* surfaces, only one tenth of it is visible above water.
- The *Nautilus* can submerge to a depth of 16,000 m (52,500 ft). When submerged, it can withstand water pressure of about 16 tons/cm^2 (19 tons/in^2), equivalent to 11 elephants balanced on a dinner plate.

The *Nautilus'* cigar shape helps it to move swiftly through the sea.

NAVIGATING THE WAY

Nemo keeps track of the *Nautilus'* position at sea by consulting his instruments. Like all 19th-century navigators, he relies on the combination of a sea chart (map), a compass, a chronometer (a very accurate clock), and a sextant. A barometer warns of bad weather.

Compass

By measuring the sun's altitude, the captain knows his latitude. He finds the longitude by comparing local time with the time at Greenwich, London, kept on a chronometer. The two readings allow him to plot his position.

Sextant

Barometer

Air reservoir holds supply for 48 hours.

Navigation room

Nemo has a valuable collection of marine plants and animals.

When not navigating the Nautilus, Nemo spends his time reading in the salon, or playing the organ.

Nemo's cabin is spacious compared to his crew's quarters.

Salon

Aronnax's cabin

Battering ram

The *Nautilus'* strong, steel spur can hole and sink enemy ships in the same way that rams on ancient Greek galleons did.

Ballast tank sits between inner and outer hulls.

Anchor

Anchor

The anchor is used to fix the *Nautilus* to the seabed.

Steel spur is the Nautilus' principal weapon.

LIVING UNDERWATER

In Verne's time, it would have been impossible to live under the sea like Captain Nemo. It wasn't until 1962 that a team of French scientists, led by Jacques Cousteau, spent a week living in a specially designed underwater house.

Habitat

Today, scientists study the effects of underwater living on people and observe marine life in submersible habitats like this.

DIVING UP AND DOWN

To make the Nautilus *submerge*, Nemo orders the ballast tanks – spaces between the inner and outer hull – to be flooded with seawater. To surface, electric pumps expel the water from the tanks by filling them with compressed air. Two diving planes on either side make the Nautilus *sink* or *rise* diagonally.

Submerging
Water pumped into the ballast tanks of the submarine makes it heavier so it sinks below sea level.

Surfacing
As water is pumped out of the ballast tanks the submarine becomes lighter and rises to the surface.

Screw
The screw, powered by the electric engine, propels the *Nautilus* forwards or backwards.

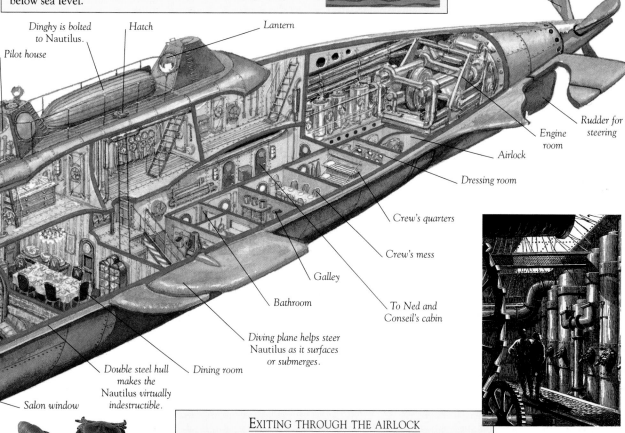

Dinghy is bolted to Nautilus.

Hatch

Lantern

Pilot house

Screw

Rudder for steering

Engine room

Airlock

Dressing room

Crew's quarters

Crew's mess

Galley

To Ned and Conseil's cabin

Bathroom

Diving plane helps steer Nautilus as it surfaces or submerges.

Double steel hull makes the Nautilus *virtually indestructible.*

Dining room

Salon window

Food from the sea
Aronnax marvels at the tasty seafood aboard the *Nautilus*. But scientists living underwater have found that food seems to change colour and consistency, and becomes virtually tasteless, under pressure.

EXITING THROUGH THE AIRLOCK

To prevent water from getting into the submarine every time someone enters or exits, divers use a special airtight compartment called an airlock. First, they put on their diving gear. Then they shut themselves in the airlock that has rubber seals on the doors. The airlock fills with seawater.

The diver enters the airlock. The door to the dressing room is sealed shut.

The diver waits as electric pumps fill the airlock slowly with seawater.

The diver can now open the outside hatch and leave the submarine.

All on electricity
The *Nautilus'* engine runs on electricity generated from seawater. First, Nemo mines coal from the seabed; this is used to heat seawater to extract its sodium. Sodium and mercury are then placed in a type of battery called a Bunsen pile, which generates the electricity that the *Nautilus* uses to power everything: to light the cabins; to make drinking water; to cook; to work the organ; and to pump air into the air reservoirs.

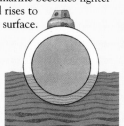

17

The captain left me alone in the salon, where I was soon joined by Ned and Conseil.

"Where am I?" Ned asked in astonishment. "The Quebec Museum?"

"It seems more like a grand hotel!" exclaimed Conseil.

"It is neither, my friends," I replied. "You're on board the submarine boat *Nautilus*, fifty metres beneath the surface of the sea."

Conseil, dedicated scientist that he was, immediately became absorbed in the hundreds of rare specimens in the display. Ned, on the other hand, was much more interested in our mysterious host: Who was he? Where did he come from? Where was he going to take us?

"I can only tell you what little I know, Ned. Captain Nemo is a fabulously wealthy man, who for unknown reasons, has decided to cut himself off from civilization. To do that, he's built this ship, a combination of museum and palace. He must be a great scientist and engineer to have accomplished such a thing. The *Nautilus* is a masterpiece and I for one am not sorry to have seen it. There are many people who'd be glad to trade places with us, if only to see such wonderful things. We must try to make the best of our situation and see what happens."

"See? How can we see anything in this iron prison? We're sailing blindly!" exclaimed Ned.

He had scarcely uttered those words when suddenly all the lights went off, plunging us into darkness.

We stood in silence, not knowing what to expect. There was a sliding noise, and two panels opened in the walls. Bright light poured into the room.

"It's the end!" cried Ned. But I could see that there was thick glass between us and the ocean outside.

What a spectacle! For two whole hours the *Nautilus* moved through schools of fish of every imaginable kind – all brilliantly lit by the *Nautilus'* powerful electric lantern. I was in ecstasy at the sight of such variety, beauty, liveliness, and colour. Meanwhile, Ned – who was only interested in fish that could be eaten – matched his knowledge with Conseil – whose only interest in fish was their scientific names.

"Look! There's a Chinese triggerfish," said Ned.

"Genus balistes, family scleroderms, order plectognaths," said Conseil. "It's like being at an aquarium."

"No," I replied, "an aquarium is a kind of cage. These fish are as free as birds in the air."

All too soon, the lights in the salon came back on, the panels slid shut, and the vision disappeared.

What a spectacle! Just outside the salon window swam an array of amazing fish.

Chapter three

AN UNDERWATER WALK

DAYS WENT BY without us seeing Captain Nemo. We were fed well, and enjoyed what liberty we were permitted. I for one had nothing to complain about. Whenever the *Nautilus* surfaced, we went up on deck to admire the view and enjoy the fresh sea breezes. And there were enough specimens in the salon to keep me busy studying for years.

1,200 leagues

Nearly a week later I found this note in my cabin:

16th November 1867

To Professor Aronnax, on board the Nautilus

Captain Nemo invites the Professor and his companions to a hunting party tomorrow in the forests of the island of Crespo.

Captain Nemo, Commander of the Nautilus

"A hunt!" cried Ned when I showed him the letter.

"So the captain does sometimes go ashore," said Conseil.

I looked at Nemo's chart. "Well, if the captain does sometimes go ashore, he certainly chooses the most deserted islands."

"Well," said Ned, "once ashore I plan to take every chance to escape!"

The next morning, the day of the hunt, the captain invited me to join him for breakfast. I asked him why he was going ashore.

"Professor," he replied, "I hunt in underwater forests."

"Underwater forests! How are we to get there?" I asked.

"On foot," replied Nemo. "Follow me if you will."

Puzzled, I followed Nemo to the rear of the submarine, where Ned and Conseil were waiting. Nemo showed us special diving suits, equipped with tanks of compressed air and regulators that would allow us to breathe naturally. We were given powerful electric lanterns and air guns that shot charged glass bullets.

Conseil and I put on special diving suits.

Conseil and I climbed into our suits, but Ned flatly refused to have anything to do with an underwater hunt. He was disappointed that this wouldn't be a chance for him to escape after all.

EXPLORING THE DEPTHS

By 1870, when Verne wrote the story, various diving suits had been invented for exploring or working on the seabed. However, scientists had yet to find better ways to allow divers to breathe underwater, and to stop water pressure from crushing them or making them ill. Although Verne's characters explore the ocean freely, it was not until the 20th century that this really became possible.

Halley's diving bell
Diving bells were the first devices for exploring the sea floor. Divers breathed the air trapped inside the bell when it sank. In 1690, Edmund Halley added extra air barrels, allowing divers to stay down for up to 90 minutes at 18 m (60 ft).

Air hose to boat

The Siebe suit
In 1837, Augustus Siebe invented the first closed diving suit. Air at the correct pressure was pumped from a boat on the surface into the diver's helmet. Siebe suit divers could stay down for up to two hours at 60 m (200 ft).

Denayrouze & Rouquayrol diving suit, 1864

DENAYROUZE & ROUQUAYROL DIVING SUIT
Verne based Nemo's diving suit on one invented by Denayrouze and Rouquayrol in 1864. It had a metal tank filled with compressed air that was attached to the diver's back. When the diver breathed in, a mechanism released the air at the correct pressure. The diver no longer had to depend on air pumped from a boat, and so had more freedom of movement.

Submarine lantern
Using his knowledge of experiments with electricity and underwater oil lamps such as this one, Verne invented the electric lantern that Nemo uses for underwater walks. Electric lights were not widely used until the 1880s.

Deep sea suit
In 1968, a new kind of suit was invented. Named after its inventor, the JIM suit keeps atmospheric pressure constant inside it so divers do not need to spend long periods of time decompressing. It can resist the pressure of water at depths of up to 450 m (1,500 ft).

Frame holds up suit when out of water.

SCUBA gear
In 1943, Jacques Cousteau and Emile Gagnan invented the revolutionary Self-Contained Underwater Breathing Apparatus (SCUBA) that automatically supplies divers with compressed air from tanks strapped to their backs. The pair also devised a rubber diving suit that allows total freedom of movement.

DIVING DANGER
As people dive down into the sea, the pressure of the water on their lungs increases. So, to breathe normally underwater, modern divers rely on compressed air – air at a higher pressure than normal. Divers must take care to come up slowly, or decompress, so as not to experience a painful condition called the bends, caused when nitrogen gas bubbles in their blood vessels.

Seaweed forest
The forest of Crespo Island is an imaginary place, but forests of seaweed do grow in the sea – along coastlines and reefs where the water is shallow.

We left the *Nautilus* through the airlock in the bottom of its hull, and a moment later, my feet touched the seabed. It was like being on another planet. I felt almost weightless as I walked across smooth sand, surrounded by strange plants, rocks, coral, shells, and fish of every colour imaginable. Long ribbons of seaweed swayed gracefully around our path, lit by a shimmering light. I was overwhelmed by the beauty of it all. I wished I could tell Conseil how I felt, but my helmet prevented me from talking.

After about an hour and a half, Captain Nemo came to a stop. He pointed to a dark mass looming ahead of us.

"That must be the undersea forest of Crespo," I thought, as we entered a forest of gigantic seaweed that towered in tall, straight columns. We explored this wonderful place, then Nemo signalled for a break. I was glad to take a rest. I even dozed off for a while. But as soon as my eyes opened they saw something so horrible that I jumped to my feet. A few metres away was a giant sea spider, ready to spring upon me! Captain Nemo stepped forward and knocked it over with his gun. The spider reminded me that even greater dangers might lurk in this beautiful forest.

We went even deeper and had to switch on our lanterns.

Soon, we arrived at a pile of gigantic blocks.

Tall columns of seaweed towered over our heads.

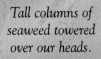

It was the base of Crespo Island, and the limit of Captain Nemo's domain, for he would not set foot on dry land.

We began our return to the *Nautilus*, taking a different, steeper route. Before long, we came to a place where the surface of the water was only ten metres over our heads. Schools of fish swam all around us. I saw the captain raise his gun to his shoulder. There was a hissing sound and a magnificent sea otter fell, stunned. Nemo's companion took the animal and we continued our trek.

The water grew shallower. The sea was so clear that I could see large birds hovering in the air above the waves. Nemo's companion aimed his gun at one of them, fired, and a huge albatross plummeted into the sea.

We were only a few minutes away from the *Nautilus* when Nemo suddenly gestured for me to get down. As I dropped to the ground, I saw a pair of dark shadows pass over me. They were two monstrous sharks, their iron jaws bristling with teeth! I was terrified, but thankfully the monsters swam away without seeing us. Half an hour later, we were safely back aboard the *Nautilus*.

Marine spider
This sea spider would come up to Aronnax's knees. It has no eyes and feeds on worms so it would not be much of a threat. It lives in cold, deep waters.

Sea otter
Sea otters live in the seaweed forests of the Pacific. Nemo kills them mainly for food, but so many 19th-century hunters were after their fur that today they are endangered.

Sunken shipwreck
Before the invention of modern diving gear and submersibles in the 20th century, it was almost impossible to explore ship-wrecks as the Nautilus does.

Chapter four

THE CORAL SEA

DURING THE FOLLOWING DAYS I saw how the crew of the *Nautilus* gathered their food. Nets were cast from the deck and drawn in heavy with fish of every kind, from eels to tuna. Some was eaten fresh; the rest was preserved.

"Professor," explained Captain Nemo, "the sea has a life of its own. It has its tantrums and its gentle moods. It has a pulse and a circulation as real as the circulation of blood in your arteries. There is always movement, always life. True existence is in the sea! Someday there will be whole undersea towns. Yet who knows if some dictator . . ."

Nemo stopped abruptly. Had he said too much? I wondered.

The sunken ship was a terrible sight!

A few days later, the *Nautilus* was once again cruising beneath the waves. I was reading in the salon when Conseil suddenly called me to the window. At first I thought the enormous dark mass was a whale. Then I realized I was wrong.

"A sunken ship!" I exclaimed.

The ship, which I later learned was called the *Florida*, was a terrible sight. I counted several drowned bodies clinging to the rigging. Saddest of all, was the figure of a woman, still holding an infant in her arms. Already the hungry sharks were approaching.

Fortunately, at that moment, the windows closed.

By early January 1868, we entered the Coral Sea. I was fascinated by the many islands that give this area its name. Billions of tiny animals working over thousands of years were slowly building up the reefs. These would eventually form islands which, in turn, might someday merge into a new continent! When I mentioned this to the captain, his only reply was, "The Earth does not need new continents, but new men!"

We passed through the Torres Straits, which separate Australia from Papua New Guinea. These are treacherous waters, shallow and full of tiny islands and hidden reefs. The *Nautilus* had to keep on the surface as Nemo guided it cautiously through this dangerous maze.

I went up on deck to watch. Then suddenly, there was a crash, and the *Nautilus* came to a stop. In a short while, Captain Nemo joined me.

"Has there been an accident?" I asked.

"An incident," he replied. "We've run aground. But we've only to wait for high tide in a few days and we'll be on our way."

When I told my friends what had happened, Ned had an idea. "Even if Nemo refuses to set foot on land, I don't see why we can't go hunting for a day on that island over there," he said.

To my great surprise, Nemo gave us permission to go ashore.

5,200 leagues

Coral reef
Aronnax admires the billions of tiny animals, called polyps, that build coral reefs. When polyps die, they leave behind thimble-shaped skeletons of limestone that gradually form a vast coral reef.

Hazardous reefs
Nemo chooses the quickest, but most dangerous, route to the Indian Ocean – through the Torres Straits. This narrow passage is filled with shallow coral reefs. Many ships were wrecked there.

With a lucky double shot, Conseil shot a pair of pigeons.

Breadfruit

Pineapple

Coconut   Bananas

Tropical fruits
Exotic fruits grow wild on tropical islands. Some, like the breadfruit, were not yet common in Europe or America. When roasted, it resembles bread.

Ned was overjoyed to set foot on dry land. Soon we were out of sight of the *Nautilus* and deep within the jungle. Tired of months of endless seafood, we gathered yams, coconuts, breadfruit, bananas, and other delicacies. Ned wanted to eat every animal in sight.

"There!" he cried, pointing to a flock of colourful birds.

"Those are parrots," replied Conseil. "They're not good eating."

"A parrot would taste like a pheasant to someone with nothing else to eat!" exclaimed Ned.

For myself, I was enchanted by the variety of birds that surrounded us: parakeets, cockatoos, even the magnificent bird of paradise.

Despite the wealth of animal life, it was noon and we still had not managed to kill anything to eat. To Ned's embarassment, it was Conseil who, with a lucky double shot, got us a pair of wood-pigeons. We made a fire and while the birds were roasting, Ned prepared some of the fruits and vegetables we had gathered. It was the best food I had ever tasted!

Hours later, we returned to the beach. Suddenly a stone fell at our feet. We looked up in surprise.

"Stones don't fall from the sky," said Conseil, "unless that was a meteorite." A second stone flew from the jungle, narrowly missing us.

"Natives!" cried Ned.

"Hurry!" I shouted. "To the boat!"

Twenty natives burst from the trees, waving spears, throwing stones, and shooting arrows. We rowed with all our might to the submarine. Once on board, I looked for Captain Nemo. To my astonishment, I found him playing the organ in the salon.

"We're being attacked by savages!" I shouted.

"Savages?" he replied. "Where in the world aren't there savages? Besides, are these people you call savages worse than anyone else?"

"Maybe not, but they're about to board us."

"There's nothing to fear," answered Nemo, calmly.

I didn't find this reassuring. Climbing to the pilot house, I saw that the natives had paddled out to the *Nautilus* in their canoes and were now clambering over the deck. Soon we would have to open the hatches to renew our air supply and, when we did, the natives would invade us. However, this didn't seem to worry the captain.

As I expected, as soon as the hatches opened, a dozen enemy faces appeared. But the first native who touched the stairrail suddenly shouted and was thrown back as though struck by an invisible force. The same thing happened to the others who tried to come down. Soon, they had all fled back to their island.

Ned, wanting to see, seized the stairrail. "A thousand devils!" he cried. "I've been struck by lightning!"

Suddenly I knew what had happened – the stairrail was giving off an electric shock. That's why Nemo had been so calm!

Native Papuan
The islanders in the story may have looked like this native of a Papua New Guinea tribe. Like most 19th-century Europeans, Ned, Aronnax, and Conseil thought the islanders were "savage" because they were so different from themselves.

The natives had paddled out in their canoes, and were clambering all over the deck.

Jellyfish
The Nautilus *passes through a school of glow-in-the-dark jellyfish like these. They have special bacteria that produce light in a process called bioluminescence.*

Chapter five

A MYSTERY

JUST AS CAPTAIN NEMO had predicted, the *Nautilus* floated off the reef with the tide. We were soon heading towards the Indian Ocean. Where would Nemo take us next?

Wherever it might be, as a scientist I was beginning to enjoy very much my journey beneath the sea. I joined the captain in gathering specimens and recording data. Conseil was delighted. His speciality was classification and he spent many hours deciding how to label our specimens. Only Ned was restless and unhappy.

One day we witnessed the most amazing and beautiful spectacle. The *Nautilus* was floating far beneath the waves and by all rights the water around us should have been as black as ink. Suddenly, however, it seemed as though the submarine was immersed in a sea of liquid light. It was living light, I discovered: several thousand tiny jellyfish surrounded us, glowing like fireflies.

We watched, enchanted, through the windows of the salon. All kinds of fish swam past, leaving glowing trails like shooting stars; best of all, an elegant porpoise, gleaming like a lantern, glided gracefully through the still waters.

Suddenly it seemed as though the submarine was immersed in a sea of liquid light.

So the days passed quickly, filled with all kinds of exciting new sights.

One day, when a storm threatened, I went up on deck as usual. Captain Nemo was studying the horizon with a telescope. He seemed very nervous, pacing back and forth, and speaking urgently to his second-in-command. Both seemed to be anxious about something. What could they have seen? I strained my eyes, but the sea seemed empty. I went to where they had left the telescope, picked it up, and started to look through it. But before I could even focus, it was snatched from my hands. I had never seen Captain Nemo look so angry! What had I done?

"Professor Aronnax," he said, "I must ask you and your companions to confine yourselves to your cabin until I see fit to release you."

"May I ask one question?"

"No."

Puzzled, I went below. I found my friends already in the cabin where we'd spent our first night. Ned and Conseil were as confused as I was when they heard what had gone on.

"Look, breakfast is waiting for us!" exclaimed Ned in surprise.

"We'd better eat," said Conseil, "for we don't know what may happen."

"You are right, Conseil," I said.

We sat down and ate in silence. Halfway through the meal the lights went out. I suddenly felt dizzy, sleepy – I could not keep my eyes open. I looked at my friends, but they had already fallen asleep where they sat. The captain had drugged our food! Above me I heard the hatch close and the sound of the *Nautilus* beginning to submerge. Then I, too, fell into a deep slumber.

Before I could even focus the telescope, Nemo snatched it from my hands.

Telescope
Sailors used a telescope to sight objects and landmarks far on the horizon. Together with other navigational instruments, such as a compass and a sextant, they could then plot their ship's position on a sea chart. Jules Verne used this telescope aboard his yacht.

Coral kingdom
Although Aronnax has already had a chance to observe corals when the Nautilus passed through the Coral Sea, he is very excited to see them up close on the underwater walk. He can admire the great variety of different coral species that grow together.

Nearby was a cross of blood-red coral.

The next day I awoke with a clear head. What had happened during the night? Were we free or were we still prisoners? I tried the door. It was unlocked. The submarine seemed deserted.

It was not until later that day that Captain Nemo finally appeared. His face was haggard with an expression of profound grief. "Are you a doctor?" he asked me.

"Yes," I said.

"Will you see one of my men?" he asked.

I agreed, and he took me to the crew's quarters where I found a man with a terrible head injury. "What happened to him?" I asked.

"Does it matter?" the captain replied. "A lever in the engine broke by accident, and it struck him. Can you help him?"

"Can he speak French?" I asked in that language.

"No," replied Nemo.

"He will be dead in two hours," I said.

At these words, tears welled up in the captain's eyes.

The next morning, I went up to the platform. As soon as the captain saw me, he asked if I would accompany him on another underwater excursion. "Of course," I agreed, and went to put on my diving suit.

Before long, Conseil, Ned, Captain Nemo, and myself were walking on the bottom of the sea. Nemo's men followed, carrying a long box of some kind. I noticed that we were in a region very different from our other underwater walk – Nemo was guiding us through a beautiful coral kingdom. After walking for two hours, the captain signalled us to halt. His men formed a semicircle around him. Nearby was a cross of blood-red coral. Suddenly, I understood everything: we were in a cemetery! The box the men carried was the coffin of their dead crewmate.

They dug the grave, lowered the coffin into the hole, and filled it with chunks of broken coral. The captain and his men knelt and bowed their heads for a moment. Then they raised their hands in a gesture of farewell and rose to their feet.

The procession returned to the *Nautilus*. As soon as I took my helmet off, I said to the captain, "At least your dead sleep quietly, out of the reach of sharks."

"Yes," he replied seriously. "Out of the reach of sharks . . . and men."

Sea turtle
Hawksbill turtles were once hunted for their meat and beautiful shells. Today this is illegal because they are an endangered species.

Clever creature
The argonaut, or nautilus, is a small spiral-shelled mollusc. Like Nemo's submarine, it can sink or swim by adjusting the amount of air inside its body.

Diving for pearls
Pearl fishing has long been an important industry in Ceylon (now Sri Lanka). Pearl fishermen used rocks to stay down while they worked. Experienced divers could hold their breath for long periods.

Chapter six

THE INDIAN OCEAN

AS TIME WENT BY, all that Ned could think about was escape. As for myself, I was in no hurry. Not only was there so much more to learn about the mysteries of the sea, but also about the mystery surrounding Captain Nemo himself. Should I hate him or admire him? Was he a victim or a villain?

These were my thoughts as we entered the clear waters of the Indian Ocean. Conseil and I spent the days watching the sea life swimming alongside the submarine, and sampled many tasty specimens of fish and sea turtle brought up in the *Nautilus'* nets.

As the submarine approached India, Ned became very excited.

"Civilization again!" he cried. "I think we might be finished with Captain Nemo's hospitality, don't you?"

"No, let's ride it out," I told him. "What harm can there be in waiting until we get closer to Europe? Then we can plan what to do."

"Well, I don't intend to wait for the captain's permission to leave!" answered the angry Canadian, storming out of the room.

I hoped he wouldn't do anything rash.

The next day, we neared Ceylon. At sunset, Conseil and I marvelled at a school of argonauts, travelling on the surface of the sea. We counted several hundred of them.

"The argonaut could leave its shell if it wanted to," I told Conseil, "but it never wants to."

"Just like the captain. He should have named his submarine the *Argonaut*."

A few days later, Captain Nemo asked me if I wanted to see the pearl fisheries of Ceylon.

"Of course I would!" I exclaimed.

"You're not afraid of sharks, are you?" he asked.

"Well, I'm not very used to them," I admitted.

"You will be in time," he said, strolling off. "Till early tomorrow morning, then."

Nemo didn't want the *Nautilus* to steer too close to the coast, so we set off at dawn in the dinghy. As we neared Manaar Island, Nemo rose and studied the sea. He signalled for us to stop, and we began putting on our diving suits.

As Nemo gave out daggers for our protection, I couldn't stop thinking about the man-eating sharks that infested these waters. Luckily, all the way to the pearl beds, I never saw even a hint of one – much to my relief.

To reach the pearl fisheries, we set off at dawn in the dinghy.

Nemo showed Aronnax the giant pearl he was growing.

Rare beauty
Pearls form when a foreign object like a grain of sand gets stuck inside an oyster. The oyster then covers the object with nacre, a pearly material from its shell. Natural pearls like Nemo's are rare; now most are grown artificially.

Terrifying jaws
Nemo may have come face to face with a tiger shark like this one. It eats anything from porpoises to tin cans, and has been known to attack people for an extra meal.

We landed on a sandbank, and followed Nemo under the waves. The sun lit the water around us so brilliantly that even the smallest objects were perfectly visible.

Swarms of brightly coloured fish fled from us like frightened birds. After walking a few miles, we found ourselves in the great pearl ground. Millions of oysters were all around us! It was an inexhaustible mine.

Ned stuffed his net with the finest ones he could find, but the captain kept on walking, leading us down deeper and deeper. Finally we came to a gloomy grotto. When my eyes became used to the dark, I saw an amazing sight: a gigantic oyster. It was two metres wide and must have weighed at least 300 kilos. With the edge of his dagger, the captain carefully pried open its shell. Inside was a pearl the size of a coconut! I reached out to touch it, but the captain stopped me and closed the shell. I understood – he was allowing it to grow larger slowly, year by year.

On our way back to the submarine, Captain Nemo abruptly gestured for us to hide behind some rocks. A large, dark shadow passed over my head and sank to the seabed. I thought it was a shark at first, but it was a man – an Indian pearl diver carried rapidly to the bottom by the stone attached to his feet. For several minutes, we watched him dive up and down, collecting oysters. Just as we were getting ready to move on, the man suddenly looked terrified and tried to spring back to the surface. Looking around, I saw what had frightened him: an enormous shark, its huge jaws opened wide. The diver swerved aside at the last second; the shark missed him, but its tail struck his chest a violent blow and he fell to the bottom, stunned. Captain Nemo rushed forward, drew his dagger, and buried it in the shark's side as it swam past.

Frozen in horror, I watched Nemo prepare to fight the shark face to face. The shark seemed to roar; blood poured from the wound in its side, turning the water red. The captain grabbed one of the monster's fins, trying to pierce its heart with his knife. Suddenly, he fell to the bottom. The shark instantly turned upon him, its gaping jaws about to bite him in two. Then, quick as thought, Ned rushed upon the shark and buried the point of his harpoon in it. Struck to its heart, the monster struggled dreadfully in its dying convulsions.

The captain pulled the half-drowned diver back to his boat, and gave the astonished man a bag of pearls. Then, Nemo motioned for us to follow him back to the dinghy, where we stripped off our diving suits. As soon as our helmets were off, Captain Nemo turned to Ned and said, "Thank you, Master Land."

"I owed you that much," replied the harpooner, and turned his back on the captain.

Once back aboard the *Nautilus*, I complimented the captain on his courage in going to the pearl diver's rescue.

"That Indian," he replied, "is an inhabitant of an oppressed country – and so am I!"

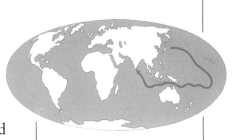

7,000 leagues

Captain Nemo buried his dagger in the shark's side as it swam past.

35

I was astonished to see a diver outside the salon window.

Suez Canal
At the time of this story, a strip of land, called an isthmus, divided the Red Sea from the Mediterranean. Until the Suez Canal was built in 1869, ships could not sail from one sea to another.

Chapter seven

CAPTAIN NEMO'S RICHES

FROM CEYLON WE CRUISED through the Arabian Sea and were soon entering the Red Sea.

"We can't be going very far," I told Ned and Conseil, "since this sea has no other outlet. The only way to get to Europe from here is to sail all the way around Africa."

"Wonderful," said Ned, unhappily. "That doesn't leave much chance for escape!"

"The last three months have gone by quickly, haven't they?" I said.

"Maybe for you," replied Ned. "As for myself, I've been counting every hour."

I was very surprised when the *Nautilus* did not turn around, but continued to sail ever further into this narrow sea. Where did Nemo plan to go? I was even more surprised at his answer: "Tomorrow we will be in the Mediterranean."

"How can that be?" I replied, amazed. "Surely the *Nautilus* cannot be so fast that it could circle Africa in one day!"

"Who told you it would have to do that?"

"Well, unless it can pass over dry land . . ."

"Or *under* it!"

The captain then told me about his great discovery: a natural tunnel – the Arabian Tunnel – that existed beneath the isthmus, connecting the Red Sea with the Mediterranean. I was amazed.

A few days later we were at the very limit of the Red Sea, in the narrow tip of the Gulf of Suez. We could go no further. The *Nautilus* submerged and we prepared to enter the Arabian Tunnel. Captain Nemo himself steered the submarine. I watched through the salon window as we entered the dark tunnel. It was very narrow and at any moment I expected we would crash into the rocky walls. However, just twenty minutes later, we were safely in the Mediterranean!

The *Nautilus* hurried on towards Crete, as though the captain were on some sort of special mission. When we came to a stop in shallow water near the island, I was astonished to see a diver signal the captain through the salon window. Ignoring me, Nemo opened a sort of strongbox filled with gold ingots. These he placed in another chest, which four crewmembers carried upstairs. What in the world was the captain doing? Where did all this gold come from? But before I could ask him anything, the captain bid me good night.

From my cabin I heard the *Nautilus'* boat being launched. The ingots were obviously being despatched to the Cretan diver. I was mystified. I knew that the people of Crete were rebelling against the Turks who had invaded their island. Perhaps the captain was helping to finance this rebellion? But why would he do this? The incident just added to the mystery surrounding Captain Nemo.

9,600 leagues

Cretan rebellion
Aronnax is referring to the Cretan rebellion of 1866. This was one of several uprisings by the people of Crete against Turkish rule. Crete was finally unified with Greece in 1908.

Gold ingots
Aronnax is astonished to see so much gold. It was worth about five million French francs (more than one million pounds), and it is only a portion of Nemo's fortune.

Oppressed peoples
Nemo appears to sympathize with oppressed peoples – first he helped the Indian pearl diver and now he seems to be financing the Cretans.

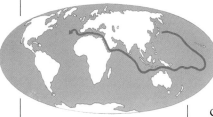

10,200 leagues

Santorini
The arc-shaped Greek island of Santorini forms a great bay – the water-filled crater of an exploded volcano. The black sand on its beaches formed when lava from a volcanic eruption reached the sea.

Volcanic activity
No one in Verne's time had ever seen an underwater volcano. Areas of volcanic activity like these volcanic vents were only discovered in 1977. Creatures never seen before were found feeding on the hot, sulphur-rich water.

A few days after the incident with the Cretan diver I was in the salon reading when I noticed that the *Nautilus* seemed peculiarly hot. Was there a fire on board? I asked the captain about it.

"No," he replied, "there's no fire. We are passing through a current of boiling water."

The panels of the salon window opened, and I gasped with astonishment. I had never imagined such a sight! The water was clouded with sulphurous smoke curling through it. I placed my hand on the glass – and quickly removed it. The window was too hot to touch.

"Where are we?" I asked.

"Near the island of Santorini. I thought you might like to witness the eruption of an underwater volcano."

"I would indeed!"

As we approached the volcano, the sea turned from white to red and the heat inside the submarine became unbearable. Scarlet flames licked through the smoky water and I was certain I could smell sulphur, even inside the sealed *Nautilus*. I felt as though I were suffocating! Broiling!

"We can't stay here!" I cried.

"I agree," Nemo said, and gave the order to retreat.

The water was clouded with sulphurous smoke curling through it.

The captain was uneasy in the Mediterranean, so we spent most of our journey there underwater. When at last we surfaced in the Atlantic Ocean, Ned, Conseil, and I were excited – we seemed so close to home!

Ned announced his plan to escape that night. He knew that we would soon be passing near the Spanish coast. "I've already told Conseil," he said. "The time is set for nine o'clock. You'll be in the library and Nemo will probably be in bed. That's when I'll get the dinghy ready."

"But there's a storm coming up," I told him. "It's going to be too dangerous!"

"I'm going whether you come or not," was his only reply.

Shortly before nine in the evening, I was nervously pacing the library, waiting for Ned's signal. Suddenly, the submarine stopped and I felt it submerging. What would Ned do? I thought with horror. Suddenly, Nemo entered the room.

"Where are we?" I asked.

He turned to the salon window and said, "On the bottom of Vigo Bay. How good is your Spanish history?"

Before I could answer the captain, he went on to tell me about the fleet of treasure ships that had sunk here more than 250 years ago. We watched as the crew of the *Nautilus* loaded chests with untold tons of gold, silver, and jewels outside the salon window. So this was the mysterious source of Captain Nemo's vast wealth!

"I don't take this wealth for myself," Nemo explained. "There are suffering people and oppressed races on this Earth, people to console, victims to avenge! Do you not understand?" He stopped then, perhaps regretting having said too much.

Remembering the Cretan diver, I think I did understand a little.

Untold tons of treasure lay waiting for Nemo to gather them up.

Lost treasure
In 1702, 23 Spanish galleons laden with riches sank in Vigo Bay. Several searches were organized in Verne's time, but much of the treasure still lies undiscovered.

Nemo's wealth
Nemo has made himself a multimillionaire by plundering the world's lost riches. Yet he doesn't want the treasure for himself; he gives it away to "deserving causes".

In 1963, an undersea volcano erupted near Iceland and formed a new island, Surtsey.

Atlantis

The Greek philosopher Plato was the first to write about the lost civilization of Atlantis. According to legend, it sank into the Atlantic without a trace when a volcano erupted there. Scientists believe that Atlantis may really have been near Santorini, the site of one of the largest volcanic explosions ever in 1645 BC.

Plaster cast of Pompeii victim

Pompeii

When Mount Vesuvius erupted in AD 79, the people of the Roman town of Pompeii were caught completely unaware. Over 2,000 died on the spot as a huge cloud of ash and gas descended upon them.

I gazed down upon a vast valley, lit by the glare of an undersea volcano. Below lay the ruins of a great city.

Chapter Eight

STRANGE PLACES

ALTHOUGH NED WAS FASCINATED when he learned about Nemo's "bank", he was more disappointed about missing his chance to escape. "We're heading away from land, now," he said, gloomily. "There'll be no hope for another chance tonight. And maybe no more chances at all."

Not long after leaving Vigo Bay, the captain surprised me by coming to my room at eleven o'clock at night. "I propose a curious expedition," he said. "It will be very long and at night, too. We'll have to climb a mountain and the roads are very bad."

"Roads?" I said, mystified, but the captain would say no more.

It was midnight when my feet touched the bottom of the sea. The water was black, but I could see a faint reddish glow in the distance. What sort of light could this be, so far underwater? We took no lanterns with us, and used the glow as our guide.

The path we took puzzled me; it seemed to be made of gigantic, smooth stones, carefully fitted together. The rosy light got brighter and brighter. What could it be? Did it come from a busy underwater city, filled with exiles like Captain Nemo?

He obviously knew his way and proceeded without the least hesitation. I followed as best I could. All around me were huge black plants and huge stone blocks, covered in vines and weeds.

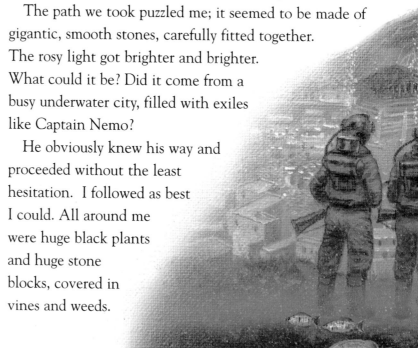

Strange, evil-looking creatures, giant lobsters, and horrible squid, scuttled in the darkness, waving their claws and antennae and tentacles at me and glaring with their glowing eyes.

It was more than two hours before we finally reached our destination, high on the side of a mountain. I gazed down upon a vast valley, lit by the glare of an undersea volcano. Below lay the ruins of a great city, its roofs open, its streets empty, its temples fallen. There was the remnant of an aqueduct, there an Acropolis or Parthenon, there the traces of an ancient harbour. It was like Pompeii, sunken beneath the waves.

Where was I? What was this place?

Captain Nemo picked up a piece of chalk and, going up to a sheet of black rock, wrote the one word:

ATLANTIS

I was amazed! The fabled lost continent of Atlantis! I had always thought it was only a myth or a legend, and there it lay before my eyes!

Nemo signalled me to return to the *Nautilus*. Reluctantly, I followed him down the mountain. We arrived back at the submarine just as the first rays of dawn were appearing.

I awoke the next day exhausted from my hike. When I checked the instruments, I saw that we were heading south. But, because the *Nautilus* was cruising underwater, I could not tell where we were.

The next morning when I woke up, the submarine had stopped. I knew we must be floating on the surface, because I could feel the *Nautilus* rocking. I went up on deck, and much to my surprise, I discovered that it was completely dark outside!

"Is that you, Professor?" I heard Captain Nemo ask.

"Yes. Where are we?"

"Underground."

"Look! A hive!" cried Ned, pointing excitedly to a nearby tree.

"Underground? And the *Nautilus* is still floating?"

"The *Nautilus* always floats. Wait a moment for your eyes to adjust and you'll see."

He was right. I soon saw that the *Nautilus* was floating in a broad, circular lake surrounded by high, rocky walls. These leaned in until they formed a domed roof over us. At the top, was a round hole through which daylight poured. The captain explained that we were inside an extinct volcano. The *Nautilus* had entered it through an underwater tunnel.

This was Nemo's coal mine. He needed coal to extract sodium for the batteries that powered the *Nautilus*. When he burned it, the escaping smoke made it look like the volcano was still active.

We were stopping for one day only, and Nemo gave the three of us permission to go "ashore" and visit the cavern. Ned came along hoping that he might be able to find some way out of the crater. We took the submarine's dinghy and left it on the beach. Then we climbed the rugged, black, volcanic rocks as high as we could. The incurving walls kept us from going higher.

Suddenly Ned cried out, "Look! A hive!"

He was right – it was a hive of bees, with honey oozing from it. We gathered up some sulphur and mixed it with some dried leaves. When this was lit, it created clouds of smoke. Soon the bees were smoked out and it was safe to take the honey. Ned scooped out several pounds and put it in his sack. He announced that he would make some honeycakes for us when we returned.

We continued our exploratory walk, and discovered that bees were not the only things flying around the volcano. Ned was eager to have some game for supper, so he tried to kill some birds by throwing stones at them. He only managed to get one of them, though.

We were exhausted when we finally got back down to the lagoon, and decided to take a nap in a little cave.

I was awakened by Conseil's shouting, "Master! Master! The tide is rising!"

The cavern was filling with water and in a few more minutes we would have drowned. Wet and tired, we returned to the *Nautilus*.

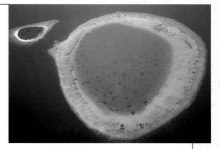

Sinking volcano
The Nautilus has sailed into a lagoon in the middle of an extinct volcano. When volcanos sink into the sea, they form a circular coral reef around a lagoon, called an atoll. Atolls occur in warm seas, not the Atlantic Ocean.

Molten rock (magma)
from a live volcano

Volcanic rock
Verne imagines that Ned, Aronnax, and Conseil are climbing up the inside of an extinct volcano. Its rocky sides were created when red-hot magma cooled.

Getting to the honey
Like modern beekepers, Ned uses smoke to tranquilize the bees so he can get to the honey they are guarding in their beehive. Man-made hives like this one make honey easier to reach.

THE OCEAN DEPTHS

After visiting the volcanic island, the *Nautilus* makes its deepest dive in the story – 16,000 metres. Today we know that this would be impossible since the deepest point on Earth is only 10,911 metres in the Pacific Ocean's Mariana Trench. However Verne's knowledge of the oceans is impressive. He knew that the world under the sea is as diverse as dry land, and is home to creatures as weird as those in myth and fiction.

SPECIAL ADAPTATIONS

Colour
The fish that live on coral reefs are brightly coloured to show predators that they are poisonous. In the deep, dark seas there is no need for bright colours, since they cannot be seen.

Butterfly fish

Camouflage
Sea animals use camouflage in various ways. Some change colour to disguise themselves; some have transparent bodies. This sea dragon has flaps of skin that make it look like the seaweed around it.

Light
Some sea creatures produce their own light through body chemicals. Jellyfish of the deeper seas can even blind their attackers with bursts of light. In the abyssal zone the only light is produced by the creatures living there.

Surface
Sea birds prey on shoals of fish; mammals, such as dolphins and whales, surface for air.

Surface

Sunlit zone
This is the most diverse area of the sea. Many marine plants and about a third of the world's fish species live on the coral reefs in this zone.

200 m
(660 ft)

Medium depths
There is less light at medium depths, and larger creatures like whales and sharks live here. Shoals of fish move from this to other regions, depending on the food available.

1,000 m
(3,300 ft)

Twilight zone
Even less sunlight reaches this zone. Creatures that live here must travel to the surface for food.

2,000 m

Size

Large animals are not always dangerous. This whale shark, is the biggest of all sharks, is no threat to people or fish. Its huge, tunnel-like mouth swallows masses of tiny plankton as it swims along.

Volcanic vents pump out hot water and poisonous minerals from the centre of the Earth. Specially adapted creatures feed on these minerals.

Small fish
Goatfish, which feed on the smallest creatures, are themselves food for larger fish and mammals.

A shoal of goatfish

Large fish
Large fish and mammals like this bottlenose dolphin feed on shoals of small fish. They in turn are often eaten by sharks.

Plankton
Plankton – the millions of tiny plants and animals that float in the sunlit zone – are the most basic source of food in the food chain.

THE FOOD CHAIN

Animals and plants that live in the ocean are dependent on each other for food. Larger creatures feed on smaller ones, which in turn eat even smaller ones. The smallest animals feed on marine plants. This system is called a food chain.

Deep-sea dweller
Marine life has adapted to life at different depths of the oceans. Creatures in the upper levels get plenty of food, whereas those of the deep sea have to survive on leftovers that float down from above. Angler fish, for example, make the most of the scarce food available by having big, upturned mouths and stretchy stomachs. This one has just eaten.

The angler fish's glow-in-the-dark lure attracts prey.

Deep, open seas
These areas are very dark and very cold. Food is scarce and conditions are extreme. Sperm whales – one of the deepest diving of all whales – and giant squid live here.

2,000 m
(6,600 ft)

4,000 m
(13,000 ft)

Abyssal zone
Some of the strangest creatures on our planet live in the deepest zone. The water here is pitch black, and almost freezing; the pressure is immense.

Deep-sea fish have tiny eyes because there is little to see in the abyssal zone.

11,000 m
(36,000 ft)

Chapter nine

TO THE POLE

The fight between the baleen whales and the sperm whales was vicious.

Baleen whale

Sperm whale

Battle of the whales

There is no evidence that sperm whales actually attack baleen whales. Deep-diving sperm whales feed on squid, while baleen whales, such as humpbacks, are gentle filter-feeders that eat tiny fish.

Antarctica

It is impossible to travel all the way to the South Pole by sea, because Antarctica is an icy landmass. Verne could not know this, because the South Pole was not reached until 1911 by Roald Amundsen.

WE CONTINUED heading south in the Atlantic. Where was the captain taking us? There was nothing beyond but the South Pole itself!

As the days passed, Ned's mood grew darker and darker, and I grew increasingly worried. So you can imagine my relief when we encountered a distraction for him – a school of baleen whales. When I went up on deck, Ned was already there, stamping his feet in his impatience. Neither of us could believe it when Captain Nemo refused to allow Ned to get his harpoon.

"What would be the purpose?" the captain asked. "We don't need whale oil. It would be killing for killing's sake. You whalers are driving these animals to extinction. Leave them alone. They have natural enemies enough to worry about."

We soon discovered what these might be. The herd was being followed by a school of sperm whales. Nemo felt very differently about these. "They are cruel creatures, nothing but mouth and teeth," he told us.

But to Ned a whale was a whale, and he was very excited at the prospect of a hunt – until he learned that the captain meant to use the *Nautilus* as his weapon.

The fight between the baleen whales and the sperm whales had just begun when the *Nautilus* joined them. Under the captain's hand, the submarine tore the sperm whales to pieces. Ned was disgusted with such gruesome slaughter and called the captain a butcher. They parted even worse enemies than before.

As more and more icebergs surrounded us, I became certain that Nemo meant to aim for the Pole. I knew that he had never reached it before; he was mad to put us all at such risk!

It wasn't long before Captain Nemo had to use the submarine as a battering ram to break through the floating ice. I wondered what would happen if we became trapped. Surely, we would not be able to go further when we reached the ice shelf itself. But nothing would deter Captain Nemo from reaching the Pole. He planned to dive far *beneath* the ice, where he was convinced there was open sea.

"We'll have to travel for several days under the ice," he told me. "But don't worry – the *Nautilus'* powerful spur will easily break through the ice at the South Pole."

I hoped he was right. Yet each time Nemo tried to surface, the ice was too thick to break through. Days went by and I began to fear that we were doomed to suffocate. At last, on 19 March, we succeeded in surfacing. We were in an open sea surrounding the South Pole!

To measure whether we were at the Pole itself, we had to wait for the stormy weather to clear. But time was running out. March 21 was the last day of the equinox, and the sun wouldn't rise again for six months. On that day, Nemo, Conseil, and I rowed to the ice-covered, rocky shore. We climbed a nearby peak, and waited anxiously. At noon exactly, the sun came out so Nemo could take his measurements. "The South Pole!" he announced.

"In whose name do you claim it?"

"In my own!" he replied, and raised his black flag.

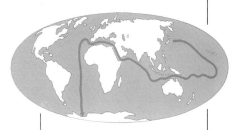

13,600 leagues

Pirate flag
Nemo's flag is black like a pirate's. This is a symbol of his rebellion against society and the international laws that govern it.

Nemo claimed the South Pole in his name.

We didn't remain long at the Pole, and were soon on our way back north. I expected the return trip to be as uneventful as the first journey, but the next morning I was awakened by a violent crash. I made my way to the salon with difficulty because the *Nautilus* was tipped so far over. Ned and Conseil were already there, but they didn't know what had happened. Captain Nemo finally arrived.

"An incident, sir?" I asked him.

"No, an accident this time."

He explained that an iceberg had overturned, trapping the submarine beneath it. We were inside a kind of ice cavern, with no way out. Captain Nemo tried ramming the *Nautilus* into the ice at full speed, but it was too solid. We were prisoners!

Wall of ice
The Nautilus *has accidentally hit an iceberg, toppling it over. It is now trapped between the polar pack ice and the overturned iceberg, hundreds of metres thick. Icebergs can tower up to 45 m above water, one-tenth of their total size.*

We took shifts working in diving suits, digging at the ice. But it seemed to freeze faster than we could cut it away.

We reacted in typical ways: Ned with anger, banging his fist on a table, Conseil was quiet, and I looked to the captain, who was deep in thought. Finally, he spoke.

"We only have two days' supply of air in the tanks. We must find a way to escape within that time."

The captain took soundings to measure the thickness of the ice around us. Above and on the sides it was hundreds of metres thick. The ice beneath the *Nautilus*, however, was only ten metres thick. If we could cut a hole the size of the submarine it would drop through.

We took shifts working in diving suits, digging at the ice. The work was unbelievably difficult and exhausting. Each time I returned to the *Nautilus*, I noticed that the air seemed to be a little worse. At the rate we were going, I calculated that it would take five days to cut a hole big enough. All we could do was try to work harder and faster.

The lack of oxygen made it more and more difficult to work. The ice seemed to freeze faster than we could cut it away. It was closing in on us. I felt dizzy, and my head ached. I knew that it would be impossible to break through the ice in time.

"We have to do something drastic," the captain told me.

"What?" I asked.

Captain Nemo reflected silently, then murmured, "Boiling water! That should stop the water from freezing and trapping us in."

Nemo ordered boiling water to be pumped onto the ice around the submarine.

Sure enough, the temperature outside began to rise. We continued digging until only four metres of ice were left beneath the *Nautilus*. By then, we could barely breathe. Captain Nemo decided the pickaxes were too slow. He ordered everyone inside. The tanks were filled with water, and the *Nautilus* settled into the hole we had dug. Soon, there was a cracking sound. The ice shattered and the *Nautilus* fell through. At last, we were free!

At full speed we rushed for the surface and broke through the ice like a leaping whale. The hatches were thrown open and pure, fresh air flooded the submarine. Conseil and Ned carried me, half passed-out, up to the deck.

"My friends," I gasped, "we must stick together no matter what!"

Chapter ten

THE GULF STREAM

17,200 leagues

Monstrous squid
No one has ever seen a live giant squid. Verne based this incident on stories he had heard and on pieces of squid fishermen had found in their nets.

Giant squid have ten arms and two tentacles; large suckers help them to capture prey. This rare specimen, found near New Zealand in 1996, is 8 m (26 ft) long, and weighs one ton.

LIKE A PRISONER fleeing his prison, the *Nautilus* rushed north, away from the polar regions. In a few weeks we found ourselves in the warm waters near the Bahamas. As we cruised past vast cliffs covered with seaweed forests, Ned, Conseil, and I argued about the possibility of real undersea monsters. I suggested that caves in the cliffs would be the perfect hiding places for giant squid or octopi. Our discussion was interrupted when Conseil suddenly pointed at the window and cried out, "Master! Look at that!"

To our horror, "that" proved to be an enormous squid. Its body was ten metres long and its eight writhing tentacles even longer than that. Between the tentacles was a vicious-looking beak.

"Look! There are six more!"

At that moment the *Nautilus* suddenly came to a stop. Captain Nemo came into the salon. "One of the squid has jammed the propeller. We'll have to surface and fight them – man to beast."

"Can't you use the guns with the electric bullets?" I asked.

"No, they are powerless against squid. We'll have to attack them with hatchets. Ned can use his harpoon."

As soon as the hatch was opened, a huge tentacle snaked down the steps. Nemo cut it off with a single blow. Before we knew it, a tentacle the size of an elephant's trunk came writhing through the hatch and snatched up one of the crew. We rushed onto the deck, where we saw the poor man being waved in the air like a trophy. "Help! Help!" he cried in French. The monster was fast carrying him towards its razor-sharp beak. Conseil, Ned, and I ran to his aid, but we were blinded by a thick cloud of black ink.

When our sight finally cleared, both the squid and

the man were gone. But there was little time for grief: we were surrounded by giant squid. Their enormous arms were everywhere! How can I describe such a battle? Blood and ink ran in rivers from the deck as we wrestled pell-mell with these horrible beasts. Suddenly, Ned was caught by a powerful tentacle and drawn towards the sharp, snapping beak! He was about to be bitten in two when Nemo's axe struck the squid right between its enormous jaws. The lifeless creature sank beneath the waves and the battle was over.

"I owed you that," the captain said.

Ned bowed his head without replying. Nemo gazed into the sea that had swallowed up so many of his crew, and great tears gathered in his eyes.

Blood and ink ran in rivers as we wrestled pell-mell with the giant squid.

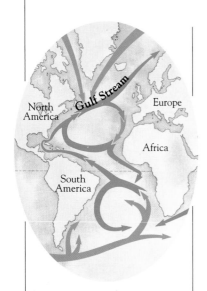

Warm currents

Cold currents

The Gulf Stream

The Nautilus *is following a well-known ocean current named the Gulf Stream. It carries warm water from the Caribbean, up the east coast of North America to Europe.*

Men laying the transatlantic cable on the *Great Eastern*

Transatlantic cable

In Verne's time, messages were sent from America to Europe by telegram. These were transmitted via the transatlantic cable, laid on the seabed by the steamship Great Eastern in 1863, and again in 1866.

We saw little of Captain Nemo after that. The mood aboard the *Nautilus* as it followed the Gulf Stream across the Atlantic towards Europe was somber. Ned came to me one day, worried.

"I'm afraid we're heading for the North Pole now," he said. "Right now we're not far from Canada. I want you to ask the captain to set us free there."

"I'll ask him tomorrow," I said.

"Today," Ned insisted.

He left me no choice. I went to find Captain Nemo. He was working in his cabin and was none too happy at the interruption.

"This book I am working on contains the story of my life and my studies. It will be sealed in a watertight box. The last man left on the *Nautilus* will throw it into the sea."

"Such wonderful secrets might be lost forever that way! Why not give the book to me, and let me and my friends go?"

"Never!"

"Then you intend to keep us here forever?" I asked.

"I answered that question seven months ago!" Nemo replied, his face twisting with anger.

"If we are prisoners, then we have the right to escape!" I retorted.

"Have I ever denied that?" he asked impatiently.

There was no use in arguing. Ned was ready to escape that very night. However, all day the wind had been rising and torrential rain was falling. As we passed Long Island, a fearsome hurricane arose, preventing any thought of escape.

Captain Nemo rode it out on deck, surrounded by howling winds, flickering lightning, and mountainous waves. He seemed to be defying the elements to destroy him. I joined him for a short while, strapping myself securely to the deck. But when lightning threatened to strike us, I fled below. Nemo finally came down at midnight, and ordered the *Nautilus* to submerge.

I was surprised to find that beneath the waves there was no sign of the tempest that raged above us. Unfortunately, the storm had driven us away from land. The *Nautilus* cruised submerged, following the transatlantic telegraph cable that connected America and Europe. In those days, we saw less of Captain Nemo than ever.

Captain Nemo rode out the
storm on the deck, as
though he were defying the
elements to destroy him.

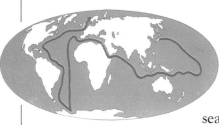

20,000 leagues

As we neared Europe, the *Nautilus* began circling, as though searching for something. When we finally surfaced, I saw Captain Nemo on deck, taking his bearings. He lowered his sextant and said, "It is here." He motioned for us to follow him.

We went below. The *Nautilus* submerged, and the salon windows opened. Nearby, I saw the enormous hulk of a sunken ship.

"That ship," explained Captain Nemo, "once carried the bravest men in the French navy. Rather than surrender to the English in 1734, its 356 sailors preferred to go down with their ship. Its flag nailed to the poop, it went down to the cry of 'Long live the Republic!'"

"It's the *Avenger*!" I exclaimed.

"Yes! The *Avenger*! A good name!" muttered Captain Nemo, folding his arms.

A dull *boom* greeted us when we returned to the surface a few minutes later. I had just gone up on deck. Ned and Conseil were

There was a terrific shock as the Nautilus *rammed the warship at full speed.*

already there. "What was that noise?" I asked.

"A gunshot," cried Ned, pointing excitedly.

Steaming rapidly toward us was a warship. It bore no flag.

"It's a man-of-war," said Ned, "and I hope it sinks this cursed *Nautilus*!"

There was another *boom* and a moment later an explosion soaked us in spray. "They must think we are the mysterious sea monster!" Conseil cried.

"But can't they see that there are men on it?" I asked.

"Maybe," offered Ned, "it is because of that."

That must be it! It must be known all over the world by now that the "monster" is really a submarine boat. Every nation must be hunting us down. Now I realized what that "shock" had been that

French and British warships fight a fierce naval battle.

Naval battle
The Avenger *was an 18th-century French warship that fought many bloody battles against the British. Just like its crew, Nemo would prefer to go down with the Nautilus than surrender to the enemy.*

had killed the man we had buried in the coral cemetery: while we had been lying in a drugged sleep, Nemo had rammed and sunk a ship!

Ned waved to the approaching warship.

Captain Nemo rushed up and knocked him down. "Fool!" he cried. "Do you want to be the next victim of the *Nautilus?*" He turned towards the mysterious ship. "Cursed nation!" he cried. "You know who I am! I don't need to see your flag to know you!"

The captain unfurled his own flag. At that moment another shot struck the hull of the *Nautilus*, rebounded off its side, and was lost in the sea.

"Get below!" roared Nemo. "I'm going to sink that ship!"

"You will not!" I cried.

"I *shall*! Don't dare to judge me! I am the law and I am the judge! I am the oppressed and there is the oppressor! Through him I have lost all that I loved – country, wife, children, father, and mother! All that I hate is there!"

Nemo did not attack the ship just then. Instead, he lured it away. I understood – he didn't want its bones to mix with those of the *Avenger*. Ned told me that this was the time to escape and I was forced to agree with him. But, just as we were preparing to climb to the deck, the *Nautilus* began to submerge. A few metres below the surface, the submarine began to accelerate. It trembled like a living thing. A terrific shock rattled through the *Nautilus* as it passed through the warship like a needle through cloth. I ran to the salon window. The sinking ship was only ten metres away. It was a horrible sight, but I couldn't tear my eyes away from it: the water was filled with struggling, drowning bodies. Suddenly the warship exploded. The window closed.

I went to Captain Nemo's room. He was sitting silently, gazing mournfully at a portrait of a young woman and two children. Clutching the picture, he fell to his knees, sobbing.

The Avenger

Nemo has lost everything to an enemy nation, whose identity Verne does not reveal. Nemo sees himself as the avenger – of his country and of his family.

He was sitting silently, gazing mournfully at a portrait of a young woman and two children.

I felt a horror of Captain Nemo. Whatever had been done to him, how could he claim the right to take such vengeance? Worse, he had made me a witness, if not an accomplice. It was too much to bear. I left the captain to his tears.

Where would the *Nautilus* go now? I wondered. I only knew that we were heading north at top speed.

One night I was awakened from terrible nightmares by Ned whispering, "We are going to escape!"

"When?"

"Tonight!"

Ned told me that land was nearby, though he didn't know what country it was. He planned to take the *Nautilus'* dinghy. He had already stocked it with food and water. The sea was rough, but he didn't foresee any real difficulties. Awed or depressed by the sinking of the warship, the crew seemed to pay little attention to what we did. We hadn't seen Nemo for a while, either.

The Nautilus, *spinning like a top, was being drawn to the bottom – and us along with it.*

"I'm ready," I said grimly.

While Ned and Conseil went on deck, I decided to take a last look at the *Nautilus* and its treasures. I heard the sound of the organ. Captain Nemo was in the salon, playing a tune of infinite sadness. What if he should see me? Our escape would be finished.

Yet, as I crossed the big room, I might have been invisible. I was about to open the door to the library when Nemo stopped playing. Tears were streaming down his face and I heard him murmur through his sobs, "Almighty God! Enough! Enough!"

They were the last words I ever heard him utter. I hurried up to the deck where Ned and Conseil had the boat ready. We climbed in and Ned prepared to set us loose. The sea was in a turmoil. Huge waves crashed around us.

"It's the maelstrom!" I cried.

The maelstrom! Now I knew where we were: off the northern coast of Norway, where tides and currents create an enormous whirlpool, one so large and so powerful that no ship had ever escaped it. The *Nautilus*, spinning like a top, was now caught in that great funnel and was being drawn to the bottom – and us along with it.

"Hold on!" cried Ned, "if we keep with the *Nautilus*, we might be safe . . ." But he had hardly spoken when, with a crash, the dinghy was torn from the submarine and hurled away like a stone from a slingshot. Something struck my head and I fell unconscious.

When I awoke, I was safely on dry land. We had been rescued by a Norwegian fisherman. While we waited for a steamship to arrive that would carry us home, I wondered what had become of the *Nautilus*. Did it escape the maelstrom? Does Captain Nemo still live? Does he still pursue his terrible vengeance? Will the waves someday carry to us his journal, so that we will at last learn his secrets? I hope so. I also hope that the *Nautilus* and its captain still live and that the scientist and explorer will have replaced the judge.

The maelstrom
This is a powerful circular current that occurs off the northern coast of Norway. Ships can run into serious trouble if they get caught up in this whirlpool.

20,000 LEAGUES

When Aronnax, Ned, and Conseil join the *Abraham Lincoln* in New York, they have no idea what a spectacular journey is in store for them. None of them expects to discover that the monster is a submarine, let alone to join it. Aboard Nemo's indestructible *Nautilus*, the characters take a whirlwind tour of 20,000 leagues (60,000 nautical miles) *around* the world. This would have been unheard of in Verne's time, when the farthest a submarine had travelled was 27 leagues (80 nautical miles).

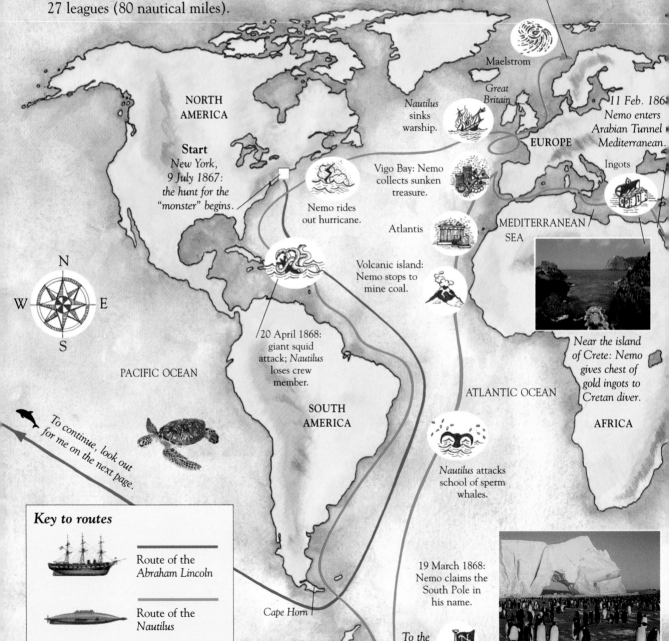

22 June 1868: Escape at last! Nautilus gets caught up in the maelstrom near Lofoten Islands, Norway.

Maelstrom

Great Britain

Nautilus sinks warship.

EUROPE

11 Feb. 1868: Nemo enters Arabian Tunnel Mediterranean.

NORTH AMERICA

Start
New York, 9 July 1867: the hunt for the "monster" begins.

Vigo Bay: Nemo collects sunken treasure.

Ingots

Nemo rides out hurricane.

Atlantis

MEDITERRANEAN SEA

Volcanic island: Nemo stops to mine coal.

Near the island of Crete: Nemo gives chest of gold ingots to Cretan diver.

N
W   E
S

20 April 1868: giant squid attack; Nautilus loses crew member.

PACIFIC OCEAN

SOUTH AMERICA

ATLANTIC OCEAN

AFRICA

To continue, look out for me on the next page.

Nautilus attacks school of sperm whales.

Key to routes

Route of the *Abraham Lincoln*

Route of the *Nautilus*

19 March 1868: Nemo claims the South Pole in his name.

Cape Horn

To the South Pole

ANTARCTICA

WHO WAS CAPTAIN NEMO?

Although there are many clues in 20,000 Leagues Under the Sea, Verne did not reveal the identity of Captain Nemo until he wrote The Mysterious Island *in 1875. In this novel, readers meet the young Nemo, Prince Dakkar, who is the son of an Indian rajah (ruler).*

Captain Nemo

Patriotic Indian

Prince Dakkar spends his youth fighting for Indian independence from Great Britain. In the story, the British government offers a reward for his assassination. When no traitors offer to kill him, the prince's parents, wife, and children are killed in his place.

Indian troops rebel against the British.

Escape to the sea

Devastated by his loss, Prince Dakkar flees from India. On a desert island, he builds the magnificent *Nautilus*, and takes to the seas in search of freedom. As Captain Nemo, he explores the oceans, and helps other freedom fighters. As we see when he sinks the warship, he never loses his desire for revenge against the British.

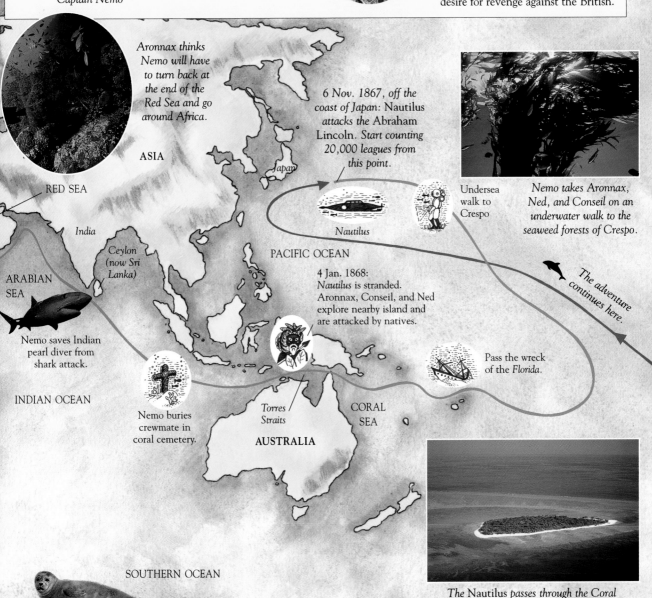

Aronnax thinks Nemo will have to turn back at the end of the Red Sea and go around Africa.

ASIA

RED SEA

India

Ceylon (now Sri Lanka)

ARABIAN SEA

Nemo saves Indian pearl diver from shark attack.

INDIAN OCEAN

Japan

6 Nov. 1867, off the coast of Japan: Nautilus attacks the Abraham Lincoln. Start counting 20,000 leagues from this point.

Nautilus

Undersea walk to Crespo

Nemo takes Aronnax, Ned, and Conseil on an underwater walk to the seaweed forests of Crespo.

PACIFIC OCEAN

4 Jan. 1868: Nautilus is stranded. Aronnax, Conseil, and Ned explore nearby island and are attacked by natives.

The adventure continues here.

Pass the wreck of the *Florida*.

Nemo buries crewmate in coral cemetery.

Torres Straits

CORAL SEA

AUSTRALIA

SOUTHERN OCEAN

The Nautilus passes through the Coral Sea, where Professor Aronnax admires coral islands and colourful reef fish.

SUBMARINES

For thousands of years, people could only speculate about what lay beneath the oceans; the deepest anyone could dive was a few metres. New technology led to the development of vessels called submarines that could travel beneath the sea. By the time Verne wrote *20,000 Leagues Under the Sea* in 1870, several craft had been launched. His *Nautilus* inspired inventors, and also anticipated today's submarines.

Unknown depths
A legend tells that Alexander the Great, (356-323 BC) had a glass barrel made so he could observe the wonders of the undersea world.

EARLY SUBMARINE INVENTIONS

To navigate underwater, a sealed chamber was needed. The first submarine was built in 1620 by a Dutch inventor, Cornelius van Drebel. It had oars, and could submerge only four metres. Subsequent craft were mostly hand-powered: the person inside turned a crank that propelled the submarine.

Crank

The Turtle
The one-person wooden submarine, the *Turtle*, was the first submarine to be used in warfare – during the US War of Independence in 1775. It did work underwater, but there was very little air inside and so it could only submerge for a few minutes.

INVENTIONS IN VERNE'S TIME

By the 1860s, scientific advances resulted in more reliable submarines. Inventors tried steam power, but this was not practical underwater; subs ran out of steam after a few miles. In 1886, the first electrically-powered submarine, also named the Nautilus, *was invented. Unlike Nemo's* Nautilus, *it had to recharge its batteries after every 80 miles.*

Verne's inspiration
Verne may have been inspired by the French vessel *Le Plongeur*, built in 1864. It was powered by compressed air, but soon ran out of air when launched. Like Verne's *Nautilus*, it had a dinghy and a spur at the front.

The Hunley
The submarine *Hunley*, named after its designer, was one of several used to fight the American Civil War (1861-65). It was so badly built that it sank several times before going into action. When it finally attacked an enemy ship, it was destroyed by the explosion.

Fantastic inventions
The 19th century was a time of great new developments in technology. Scientists, artists, and writers like Verne dreamed of machines that could do anything – including cruise under the sea in style.

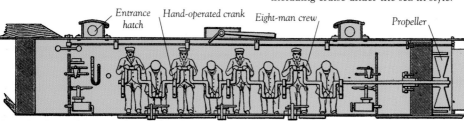

Entrance hatch — *Hand-operated crank* — *Eight-man crew* — *Propeller*

HOW DEEP CAN WE GO?

Sponge divers holding their breath: 15 m (50 ft)

SCUBA divers with their own air supply: 50 m (164 ft)

JIM suit: 400 m (1,312 ft)

Deepest-ever dive using air pumped from the surface: 500 m (1,640 ft)

Barton and Beebe's Bathysphere: 923 m (3,028 ft)

Alvin, a two-person deep-sea submersible: 3,810 m (12,500 ft)

Unmanned robot Jason Jr: 4,000 m (13,120 ft)

French submersible, Nautile: 6,000 m (19,685 ft)

The Trieste holds the record for the deepest dive: 10,911 m (35,800 ft)

Nemo's Nautilus: an impossible 16,000 m (52,500 ft)

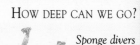
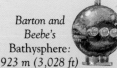

From the 1900s, submarines were developed for warfare and underwater exploration. New submarines were used successfully in both world wars, while pioneering explorations in peacetime greatly increased scientists' knowledge of the oceans. And at last an even more powerful vessel than Nemo's Nautilus was successfully launched – the nuclear submarine.

Bathysphere
The first craft for peaceful ocean exploration was built in 1934 by two Americans: William Beebe and Otis Barton. Beebe descended a record 923 metres in their *Bathysphere*, a steel sphere suspended by cables. He reported seeing such strange deep-sea creatures that no one believed him at first.

The Bathysphere's round shape could withstand water pressure at great depths.

Deepest ever dive
Designed by Auguste Piccard and manned by his son Jacques, the *Trieste* holds the record for the deepest dive. In 1960, it reached the deepest point on Earth, the bottom of the Mariana Trench in the Pacific Ocean, 10,911 metres down. This is about 2,000 metres deeper than the highest peak of Mount Everest would be if it were turned upside down. Piccard reported that life did exist in the Trench.

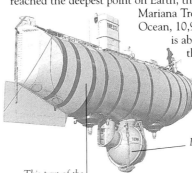

Piccard sat in the small sphere underneath.

This part of the Trieste is a buoyancy tank that works like a hot-air balloon.

American nuclear submarine: USN Dallas

nuclear submarines
he first nuclear submarine, the USS *Nautilus*, was launched in 54 by the US Navy. It had its own nuclear reactor, so it could vel fast, dive deep, and, most importantly, go long distances thout refuelling. But, unlike Nemo's *Nautilus* which could stay sea indefinitely, nuclear subs have to return to port for food d supplies. Verne's *Nautilus* can do almost most everything a clear submarine can, but nuclear subs, armed with missiles and rpedoes, are much more powerful war machines.

EXPLORING THE OCEAN

The ocean covers two-thirds of the Earth's surface, yet scientists have only explored about two percent of it. When people first began charting the ocean, they relied on ships' reports and stories about unknown and terrifying creatures.

Verne spent hours studying drawings like this one of coral by Marsigli.

First investigations
In 1725, an Italian named Marsigli carried out the first formal observation of ocean life. Over 100 years later, in 1861, Matthew Maury used ships' observations to compile a chart of ocean currents and winds. Maury's work greatly influenced Verne.

Oceanography is born
The formal study of the oceans – oceanography – began in 1872 when the English ship *Challenger* set off on a four-year journey. Observations on sea currents, temperatures, and marine life filled 50 volumes that are still used today.

The submersible Alvin helped to explore the wreck of the Titanic in 1985.

The very bottom
Finally, in the 1960s, small craft called submersibles were invented. They allowed people to explore the ocean at depths where other submarines would be crushed.

VERNE'S VISION

Jules Verne (1828-1905) was fascinated by frontiers. Although he did not travel much in his lifetime, his characters went all over the world, to outer space, to the centre of the Earth, and under the sea. He imagined what these places were like, then added his own scientific knowledge to create a new kind of story called science fiction. Verne was way ahead of his time – often with astounding accuracy, he predicted what life would be like in the future and many of his imaginary machines have since been developed by modern science.

Around the World in 80 Days (1873) inspired adventurers to race around the world. By the end of Verne's lifetime, the record was only 54 days.

SCIENCE-FICTION WRITER

Like Nemo, Verne loved the sea. He was born by the French seaside, in Nantes, and when he was eleven, tried to run away to sea. His father made him study law, but Verne wanted to be a writer. Success came in 1856, when Five Weeks in a Balloon was serialized in an educational magazine. It was to be the first of more than 60 novels.

Inspired storytelling
Verne's stories transported his readers to exciting, unknown places they never dreamed of visiting. In this caricature, Verne is shown leaning on the globe, holding the Moon, dreaming of exploring faraway worlds.

Verne's globe

All around the world
Geography and exploration were Verne's first loves. He kept this globe aboard his yacht, where he wrote many of his novels. Verne used it to trace some of the routes travelled by his characters.

Literary success
Verne's stories were first serialized in an educational magazine, then bound in handsome editions such as these.

Family home
In 1856, Verne married a young widow with two children. Together they had another son, and settled in this elegant family home in Amiens, northern France. It was during this period that Verne travelled to America on the steamship *Great Eastern*. Verne died in Amiens in 1905.

Exciting adventure stories
As Verne's popularity as a writer increased, his publisher collected his works in a series called *Extraordinary Voyages*. This postcard illustration shows Verne in the centre surrounded by two famous scenes from his books: the shark attack in *20,000 Leagues Under the Sea* and Top the dog's encounter with the snake in *The Mysterious Island*.

Verne would perhaps be surprised at how much is still to be learnt about the oceans. This vast, untapped resource may in the future provide underwater homes, new medicines, food, and water. But the oceans are under threat. Since Verne's time, they have been damaged by overfishing, tourism, and pollution. Now international laws help to protect the ocean environment.

Harvesting kelp for food.

When oil from an oil spill covers birds' feathers, they are no longer waterproof. Water soaks into them and the birds drown.

Farming the sea

The *Nautilus'* crew was completely dependent on the ocean for food and water. Verne may have been predicting that one day we would farm the sea as we farm the land. Products such as fish, kelp, and oysters are already being farmed.

Underwater exploration

When Jacques Cousteau's film *The Silent World* was released in 1956, it was the first time many people had ever seen the depths of the oceans. Cousteau's films and underwater expeditions made many people realize the importance of preserving our precious oceans.

Endangered creatures

Rubbish dumped in the oceans and accidental oil spills are two main causes of death to sea plants and animals. Pollution affects the food chain, too. If plankton or small fish are poisoned, predators and humans who eat them may get sick or even die.

Action on film

Verne's science fiction stories make good action films. This Spanish poster from the star-studded, award-winning 1954 Disney film, *20,000 Leagues Under the Sea*, shows the *Nautilus* and its crew on an underwater walk.

Board game

This Disney game popularized the exploits of Captain Nemo and the *Nautilus*. The aim of the game is to "race your *Nautilus* to safety past the moving gunboats".

Scary giants

Verne's works inspired film makers to invent strange monsters, such as this giant nautilus that features in the 1961 film of *The Mysterious Island* (right), to thrill their public. In this scene, the nautilus is holding a man in its tentacles, much like the giant squid does in *20,000 Leagues Under the Sea*.

Acknowledgements

Picture Credits.
The publisher would like to thank the following for their kind permission to reproduce their photographs:

a=above; b=below; c=centre,
l=left; r=right; t=top.

AKG London: 8cl.
Bryan & Cherry Alexander: David Rootes 46bl.
Ancient Art & Architecture: 40cl.
Ardea London: John Clegg 45cr; Francois Gohier 45tr; Jean Michel Labat 44tl; Ron & Valerie Taylor 45tl.
Associated Press AP: Martin Hunter 50bl.
The Bridgeman Art Library London/New York: Bibliothèque Royale de Belgique, Brussels: *Alexander the Great (356-323 B.C.) from L'Histoire du noble et valliant roy Alixandre le Grant,* French (1506) 60tr; Private Collection: Howard Davie: *Sir Henry Havelock (1795-1857) at the Relief of Lucknow, 1857* from *Heroes of History* by Raphael Tuck & Son Limited 59tc.
British Museum: 39cr.
Bruce Coleman Collection: Peter Evans 59bl.
Corbis: James Amos 16br; Jonathon Blair 37br; UPI 61c.
ET Archive: 6tl, 54bl.
Mary Evans Picture Library: 12tl, 21tl, 32br, 37cr, 52bl, 60b, 60cl.
The Collection of Count Gondolo della Riva, Italy: 21br, 59tr, 60cb, 62, 63cl, cr.
Ronald Grant Archive: *The Silent World* 1956 © Jacques-Yves Cousteau 63tc, *The Mysterious Island* 1961 © Columbia Pictures 63br.
The Image Bank: 27tr; Steve Grubman 34cl; Jeff Hunter 1c.
Frank Lane Picture Agency: Treat Davidson 43br; S. Jonasson 40tl; Silvestris 57tr; D.P. Wilson 32cl.
Museum of London: 39cr.
Musée du Scaphandre, Espalion, France: L. Cabrolié 21c, 21cr.
NHPA: 23tr; James Carmichael 23cr; Kevin Schafer 28tl; David Woodfall 58cr.
National Trust Photographic Library: Andreas Von Einsiedel 14tl.
Natural History Museum: Frank Greenaway 46cl; Harry Taylor 7br.
National Maritime Museum: James Stevenson 9tr, 16bcl, 16abr.
Oxford Scientific Films: Gary Bell 45btr; Raymond Blythe 38cl; Peter Parks 44tr.
Pictor International: 25br, 59br.
Planet Earth Pictures: Kurt Amsler 21bc; Gary Bell 25cr, 30tl, 38bl; Mark Conlin 22tl, 59cr; Georgette Douwma 32tl; Krafft 43cr; Robert Lureit 63tl; Pete Oxford 58br; Doug Perrine 34bl, 59bcl; Linda Pitkin 59cl; P Rowlands 24tl; Henwarth Voigtmann 43tr.
RSPB Images: Steve Omerod 63tr.
Royal Navy Submarine Museum: 21br.
Science Museum: 17tr.
Still Pictures: Fred Bavendam 44tc.
Tony Stone Images: 48tl; Mike Stevens 58cl; Hans Strand.
TRH Pictures: 61tl.
Wildlife Conservation Society, Bronx Zoo, New York: 61tr.
World Pictures: 36bl.

Jacket: **The Collection of Count Gondolo della Riva, Italy:** front tl, inside back tl.
The Image Bank: Jeff Hunter back abl.
The National Maritime Museum: James Stevenson front tr.

Maps/additional illustrations: Lorraine Harrison; Sallie Alane Reason; Stephen Raw; Eugene Fleury; Richard Orr.

Additional photography: Andy Crawford; Ray Moller; James Stevenson; Dave King; Alex Wilson; Tina Chambers; Gary Ombler.

Dorling Kindersley would particularly like to thank the following people:

Count Gondolo della Riva; William Watson; Arthur Edwards; Lucien Cabrolié, Musée du Scaphandre, Association Musée Bibliothèque Joseph Vaylet, Espalion; John Bevan, Historical Diving Association; Jo Pecorelli, The London Aquarium; Neil Brown and David Woodcock, Science Museum; Robert Graham for research assistance; Miriam Farbey for editorial assistance; Clair Watson for design assistance; Nick Turpin for anglicization.